www.mascotbooks.com

Poe's Road Trip to Ravens Gameday

©2016 Baltimore Ravens. All Rights Reserved. No part of this publication may be reproduced, stored in a retrieval system or transmitted in any form by any means electronic, mechanical, or photocopying, recording or otherwise without the permission of the author.

For more information, please contact:
Mascot Books
560 Herndon Parkway #120
Herndon, VA 20170
info@mascotbooks.com

CPSIA Code: PRT0916A
ISBN-13: 978-1-63177-812-4

Printed in the United States

POE'S
Road Trip to
RAVENS
GAMEDAY

Written by
POE

Illustrations by
BRIAN MARTIN

It was a beautiful Monday morning in Baltimore as **POE**, the mascot for the Baltimore Ravens, woke up to start his day. After eating a healthy breakfast, Poe worked out with a few friends at the Merritt Athletic Club.

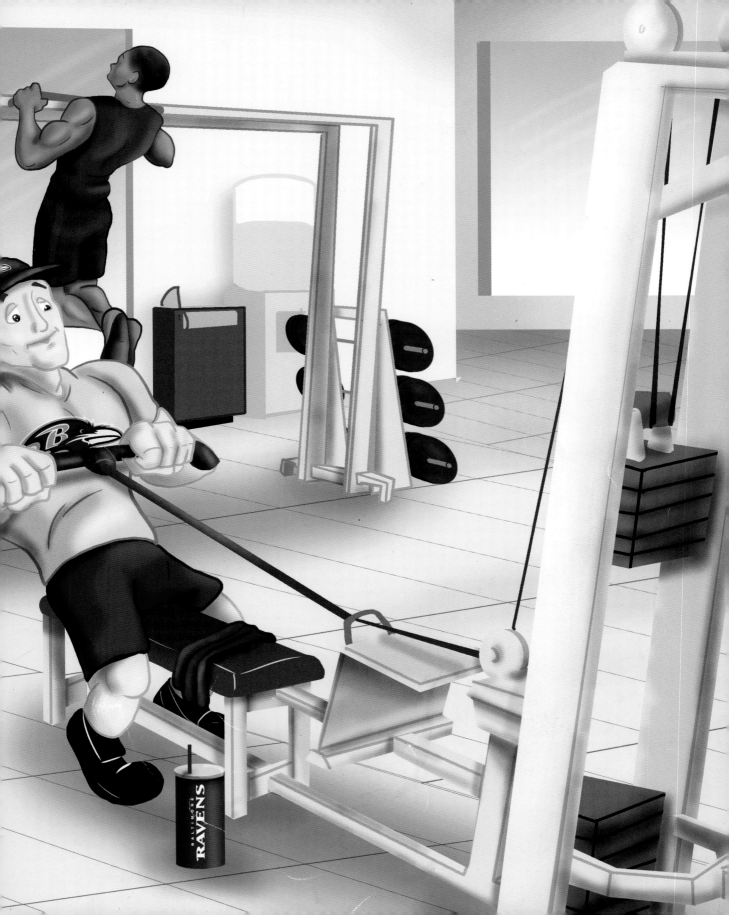

Later, Poe rode with his friends on the bookmobile to a nearby school. Poe was excited to share his favorite story, *The Raven,* with all of the students!

After Poe's reading, everyone went outside for field day. A few players from the **BALTIMORE RAVENS** were there to play a game of touch football with Poe. "I like to get up and play for 60 minutes every day!" Poe said.

On Tuesday, Poe visited Maryland's capital city, **ANNAPOLIS.**
As he toured the Maryland State House and Historic Annapolis,
Poe saw many men and women dressed in uniform. *They must be
from the U.S. Naval Academy,* he thought.

"Thank you for your service!" he said to service members
passing by.

On Wednesday, Poe spent the day in **OCEAN CITY.** He rode on a crabbing boat along Maryland's Eastern Shore, enjoying the afternoon sun.

Poe also explored the boardwalk and met many Ravens fans. There was so much to do!

On Thursday, Poe visited City Hall in Baltimore with some of the Ravens' staff members. With the season about to start, it was time to paint the town **PURPLE!**

Is my head really that big? thought Poe, as he took pictures with a family next to the giant birdie head painted on the grass.

On Friday, Poe stopped by one of his favorite places, **THE MARYLAND ZOO** in Baltimore. He'd heard about the new African penguin exhibit and couldn't wait to check it out. Poe saw two real ravens near the Penguin Coast exhibit. "Hey, I know them! That's Rise and Conquer. They help me with my mascot duties for the team!"

Walking around the zoo, Poe noticed many Ravens fans in **PURPLE,** his favorite color! Purple Friday is also his favorite day during Ravens season.

Before the game the next day, Poe wanted to visit one last place—**FORT McHENRY.** That's where American soldiers successfully defended the Baltimore Harbor from British troops during the War of 1812.

Poe couldn't believe he was standing where Francis Scott Key once stood and was later inspired to write "The Star Spangled Banner."

"I know that song!" Poe said. "We sing it before every game."

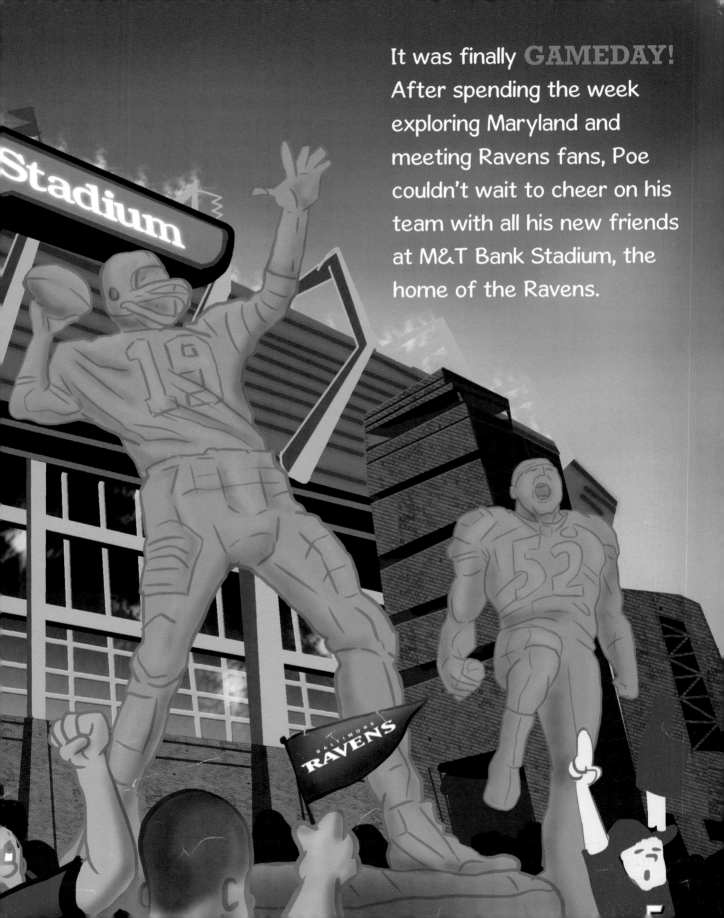

It was finally **GAMEDAY!** After spending the week exploring Maryland and meeting Ravens fans, Poe couldn't wait to cheer on his team with all his new friends at M&T Bank Stadium, the home of the Ravens.

Before the game, Poe visited RAVENSWALK for pre-game festivities. With so many fans to meet, games to play, and food stations, he didn't know where to start!

It was just about time for the game to begin! After **POE** and the Ravens ran out of the tunnel, they stood on the sidelines and sang the national anthem. As they did, Poe remembered his visit to Fort McHenry, and the song felt extra special.

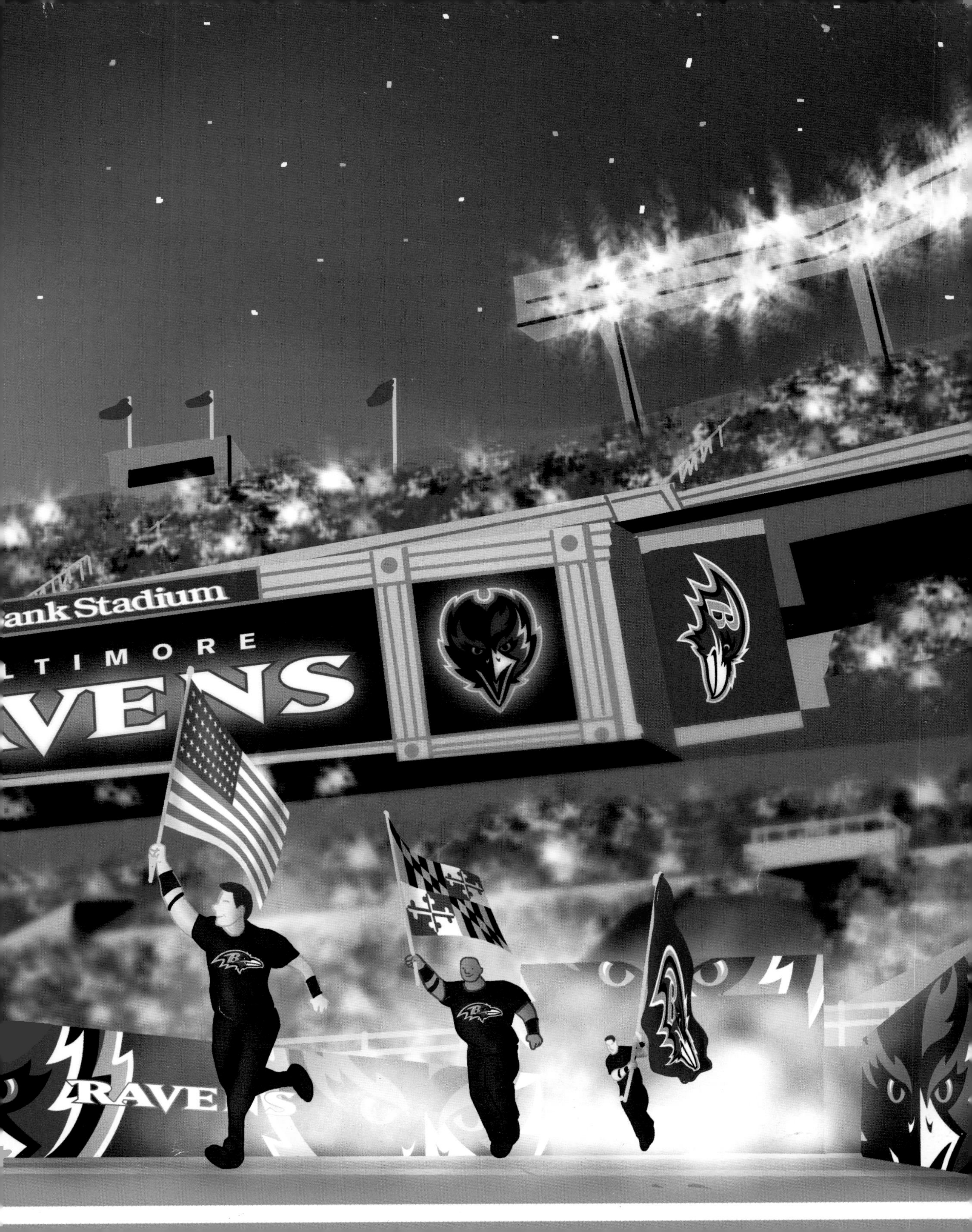
ank Stadium
LTIMORE
AVENS
RAVENS

After kickoff, it didn't take long for the Ravens to march down the field. Soon, the announcer cheered, **"TOUCHDOWN, RAVENS!"**

After playing hard against the other team, the Ravens scored another touchdown late in the fourth quarter. **THE RAVENS WON THE GAME!**

It's the perfect ending to a great week, thought Poe, as he celebrated with fans and players.

Proceeds from the sale of this book will benefit the Ravens Foundation, Inc. and its dedication to support children's literacy development efforts in Maryland.

ACKNOWLEDGEMENTS

PROJECT MANAGER: Ilsa Marden

CONTRIBUTORS: Brad Downs, Heather Darney, Brandon Williams, Rob Tune, Patrick Gleason, and Marisol Renner

Have a book idea?
Contact us at:

info@mascotbooks.com | www.mascotbooks.com